disappearing from view

Jeongmin Choi

a DSTL arts publication

disappearing from view

a DSTL Arts publication

The work in this book was written by Jeongmin "Jamie" Choi, a participant in DSTL Arts's Poet/Artist Development Program, and first printed in October, 2024 by DSTL Arts publishing in Los Angeles, CA, U.S.A.

Original Cover Art: NRPV

Original Illustrations: Jeongmin "Jamie" Choi

Cover and Book Design: Luis Antonio Pichardo

ISBN: 978-1-946081-79-7

10 9 8 7 6 5 4 3 2 1

www.DSTLArts.org

Los Angeles, CA

Thank you to all those who came together to get this chapbook released and published.

Especially to my close friends, loved ones, and family—this book you are holding is dedicated to you. I appreciate and cherish all of the encouragement I received from you all.

And to DSTL Arts and my cohort, I would like to dedicate the whole of my gratitude for accepting me into your program. Of course, this chapbook would simply not take the form it has now if it weren't for the P/AD mentorship.

And to the reader, whoever you are, having picked up this copy of my chapbook, I thank you as well. You have allowed hope to live on in me.

Table of Contents

Permission Slip for
Self-Awakening

Dear _____,

It is with great pleasure to let you know that [*Afraid Not Fellowship*] is sponsoring a trip with a big cohort of like-minded individuals. Thoroughly read this slip and fill out the form if you would like to attend.

Please note that you must agree to the following in order to attend:

- Be not afraid of the journey ahead. You will still be scared, but you have to promise that you can take another step forward, even if you go back a few steps.
- If you end up shedding tears before or after the event, you must save them for a later activity.
- Please bring bear spray.*
- If you own any garments made of polyester, please leave them at home.
- Precious fuel.

No bears will be harmed during this trip.

— — — — — — — — — **Tear Here** — — — — — — — — — —

This form must be signed by YOU by the following date:
Month:____/ Day:____/ Year:_____

You are permitting yourself to go forward, ahead. You can look back, you can see what you left behind. And that's you, staring back. Going toward what's happening before you isn't the same as leaving your past behind. Do you remember the most painful parts of what your past self has been holding onto this whole time?

All the rage, grief, joy, and feelings without words—don't forget them. This is precious fuel.

Sign here: _____

Little Miracle

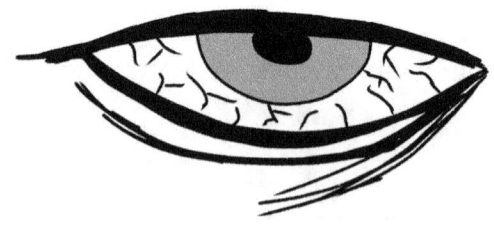

Once upon a time, there was a little apartment. A perfectly tame little place that came with rent-control.

Within the apartment lived up to 30-40 tenants. They lived in shaky harmony, as one does in a building like this one. Though there was no shortage of complaints, such as the communal dryer constantly being broken or the hallway lights flickering at the exact same time every six months, all was as well as it could be.

Until one day, the tenants began hearing noises coming from the underground parking lot. At first, the noises were small, like a car starting late at night. But it was just a little louder than that, enough to hear it in the dead quiet of the night. It rattled the underground, enough for the pots and pans to vibrate along to its tune. Then it rattled for a few beats: one, two, three, four... But it never lasted long, and, as most noise does in this city, it made its home in the little apartment, blending right in, unsuspected.

However, as the days went on, the noise continued to grow. And only in the middle of the night did it make itself known. The noise grew louder and louder, until the vibrations of it shook the very foundations of the little apartment. Books shook on its shelves; the shower curtains clattered on the metal rails; everything took a turn to react to the sound bellowing below.

The tenants took note, of course. And they escalated their complaints to management, who in turn did little but to assuage them with light-hearted words that they will notify the tenant via letter. Surely, we trust those in power to take care of it for us. But the noises continued, every night, around two o'clock in the morning. Tenants cursed aloud in frustration, unable to escape that all-too-familiar roar of what sounded like a modified engine.

And you may be asking, weren't there any witnesses to the car? And there were: as many as five people had seen a young man turn on the engine at night, testing and checking his modifications. Surely then there is no surprise, knowing that he was the sole reason for the noises that echoed deep into the night.

But, really, what can the tenants of this little apartment building do?

Every night he tweaked his car. And every night the tenants lost sleep. Their ears, forced to be subject to the abrupt sounds of the engine revving, the undeniable rumbling that vibrated the very floors themselves.

Oddly enough, neighbors noticed that, the more disheveled his appearance got, the louder his car grew.

The tenants would lay awake at night. There was nothing they could do. Noise complaints mattered little. Calling the cops had no real resolution. All they could do is pray to their chosen gods for the young man to leave, far, far away from the little apartment.

But he didn't leave. And his car only grew louder.

Tenants lost focus and dreaded going to bed, only to be jolted awake again. Every night, the cycle continued.

And this is where the "until one day" comes in.

Until one day, as the day waned into night, as the night turned a deeper shade of black, much like clicker-trained dogs, the tenants braced themselves for the dreaded bone-shaking whirring of that car-turned-abomination.

Silence.

Not a sound in the night. Not a single thing moved.

The tenants all looked in the general direction of the underground right below them, staring in bewilderment. Some sighed in relief, turning over to sleep for the first time in what felt like an eternity. And all was well again. Silence spilled over the little apartment, over the plaster walls, over the first-floor units especially, and even the laundry room nestled so quietly in the corner of the gated parking lot.

And who knows what happened to the car that went

vroom ... *vroom*

in the

middle

of the night?

I suppose I wouldn't know.

All I know is that the tenants of the building had little care in the world, and they found themselves waking one morning from what merely seemed to be a very long nightmare.

And as for the young man?

Most of the neighbors say he simply moved out one day. It is a plausible explanation, and one could say, also a miracle. An act of divine intervention. But I heard from someone who has keys to the security room on the second floor that they had looked into what could have happened to the young man. Just out of curiosity, of course.

And they found something a little odd. A few days before the noises stopped, there was someone in gray pajamas who approached the door of the young man's apartment. A young woman, from the looks of it, holding a black plastic bag in her hand. She removed from the bag what looked to be a bottle of some kind. And from that bottle she smeared a liquid substance onto her hand. Then she rubbed it on the apartment door handle. She crouched down, staring hard at the bottom of the door, as though waiting for a sign. You could make out the whites of her eyes even from the grainy footage—so eagerly did she stare.

Then, she got up and walked away. As though nothing happened.

And perhaps nothing happened. Because this is a happy ending, where all is well again, with little to no change to the little apartment. Years later, many tenants will move out, and their lives will be filled to the brim with the dramas of the day-to-day, the 9-to-5, the stress of survival. And they will, naturally, forget it all.

But no worries. When this fades into a dream, into just a wisp or suggestion of a memory, I shall remember. I will dream of the incredibly loud, horrible car, the shaking infrastructure of this building made of paper mâché, the unified anger that brewed over countless nights.

I shall treasure it all, as is my duty in the heart of this ordinary little apartment.

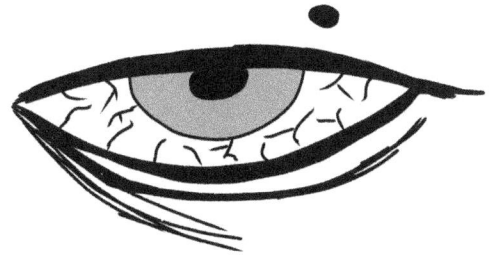

Father's Nursery Rhyme

Father, father, give me water,
Gave me distance,
Gave me power.
Sins upon the holy daughter,
Seek your roots beneath this flower.

Father, father, more than water,
Give me time, a given hour.
Under broken—
broken shower
Flood is rotting something sour.

Father, father, even water,
Leaves my eyes before the slaughter.
Focus on your inner martyr,
And may your blood shine ever brighter.

Father, father, cup of water,
Hold it high, and hold it tighter.
Consider me some kind of monster,
Easy for you and even better.

Father, father.
Come a little closer.
You avert your gaze from your only fighter.
And you take from me all the things that matter.
But worry not.

I will weep for you
When they put you under.
And I shall greet you

In the hereafter.

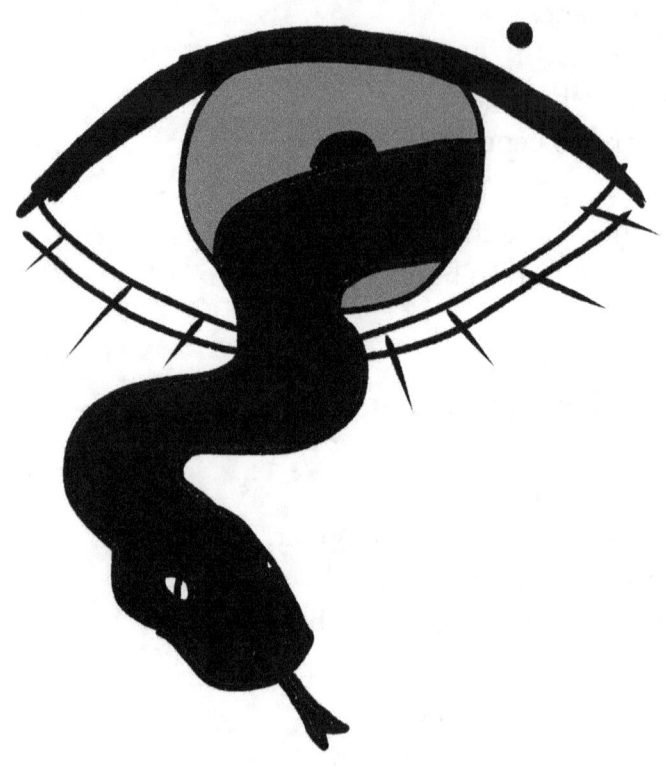

Venting

In 1992, a snake slithers across the concrete in a back alley of Seoul and enters through the pipes where the rainwater drains out of the rooftops of a building. Undetected, it follows the plumbing into a wedding dress shop on the second floor of the small building. A standalone building is already odd in this part of town where buildings stay low and are adjacent to a few shops at least, a liquor store connected to a restaurant and the like. The sign outside of this building reads, JINA'S WEDDING DRESS in a font too large. The enormous dress shop name emblazoned across such a building causes people to pause and wonder for a brief second every time they walk by. Those who ever stopped and wondered would hear just two weeks later about a strange case of an anaconda having entered the building and devouring something too big for it to swallow.

Family

I didn't realize it was so unique.

I sit at my desk, scribbling on a journal, taking for granted the way the sun shines through the windows to my right.

It is at this time, when I decide to take a meal break, that I pass by *it*.

I glance at the rattling little cage on the way out of my room. A creature I've known all my life sits in it. A hunched over thing. It taps between the steel gaps on the cage, trying to get my attention, "Hey, hey."

I ignore it as I leave to get a cup of yogurt from the kitchen.

You would think that it would try to get my attention while I'm away. But it doesn't. The creature waits for me to inevitably return to my room. And when I do, it rattles the cage.

"Hey, hey," it says. "Don't you know that it's rude to ignore people?"

It takes every bit of my strength to not point out the fact that it doesn't belong to the category called *people,* and never has in its whole life. I know that's what it wants, so I don't cast a single glance at the creature. Instead, I sit down to clock into my remote job, exchanging virtual pleasantries with my coworkers for a little bit and catch up on emails.

"Hey, hey. You had yogurt again? Aren't you sick of that shit?" The creature is now rolling around in what little space it has, banging around as it hits the metal.

—

When I was younger, I grew up with this thing making sounds in the den of my childhood home. The first time I laid eyes on it, my mom showed it to me, not with trepidation, per se, but she did tell me, "Jamie, this is our little creature. Whatever you do, we cannot let him out, but he provides protection over our house."

I stared, a little frightened and sticking close to my mom's side, taking in the look of a small rat-like creature, with what looked to be eyes covering its whole body.

"Our little creature is called Morgan." My mom gently touched my shoulder to get my attention. "Can you say Mor-gan?"

The creature turned its head toward our direction, ears perking up at the mention of its name.

"Mor," I repeated, "Gan."

As soon as I did, the creature jumped, latching onto the cage bars and making noises that resembled short, repetitive howls, the rattling of metal dispersed in between. Mom seemed pleased at the reaction, though the sounds frankly frightened me more than anything.

"Oh! Morgan is so excited to finally meet you, love."

She stooped down to my level, meeting my unsure eyes, but not looking at me, not really. "One day, you and Morgan will be great friends."

Mom turned toward the creature and left me outside of the den, while she disappeared within. I would hear laughter and joy, and I wondered what could be so funny.

Laundry Land

how have you felt about laundry recently? seen any new laundry machines? i heard they opened a new laundromat down the street from us. they have LED lights to really brighten up the space, and it is huge. i mean, you might never meet another person while doing your laundry there. i mean, you would have to shout at the other person across the enormous room for them to hear you, and even then, they might be out of range depending on your vocal projection.

my goodness, is it pristine! the coin changers are right there for you to use, and they are spic-n-span, whistle-clean, eat-off-the-floor. no, no, i am being 100% serious right now. if someone asked me, "ma'am, do you think there is a heaven or hell?" i would say, "i don't know about hell, but heaven is literally right there, ready to press and fold your denim to perfection."

these machines, these machines, you could wash a car in these things. you could wash a mattress, a loveseat, and possibly three office chairs at once. i could wash myself in these things. like shit, i would if they let me, but the staff stared at me then looked worriedly at their beautiful telephone next to their equally beautiful touchscreen interface, so i did practice some restraint. and no, i don't know what the touchscreen does. why does that matter?

look at this! the drum is the size of my bedroom. i could live in there with some amenities if they wanted to take my rent. cozy, like an alien sleeping pod. me, curled up like a chipmunk in the hollow of a tree. the "pine fresh" fragrance from an enzyme-based organic laundry detergent by a startup—it smells just like the real thing! and everlasting on my clothes. from my wonderfully damp laundry-condo, i would open the circular door every morning, and splattered along the back wall would be the most perfect view of paradise, that sweet mural of a radioactive sunset in SunnyD orange gradating into a bloom of arsenic yellow.

the whirlpool of water is magnificent. high efficiency. every setting you could imagine. oh, my god. i could cry just thinking about it. i could well up in tears at the thought of delicately changing the settings to adjust it to my laundry. deep-clean and sanitize? deep-clean and sanitize my clothes? my clothes might not even deserve to be in there, you know.

what the fuck does the "eco-friendly" setting do? i'll be honest—i don't care, and i'm pressing it.

i know. you must be thrilled for me, going and pressing the *eco* button on the brand new Laundry Land machines; and i would be, too, if i could do such a sacrilegious thing.

do you see that apartment down there?

that's where i live, and that's where my neighbor who died used to live.

my neighbor who died with no one around, as a lonely, separated husband and father whose body was found in a mountain of his own trash weeks after his passing. the poor guy bequeathed upon me and my other neighbors the precious gift of a thousand hungry bedbugs. i saw them on the ceiling. i saw them on the floor. i saw them on my windowsill. i saw them crawling into my REM cycle, stealing blood and sleep.

and what do you know? bedbugs need to be heated up to a toasty 120 degrees Fahrenheit for a good ten minutes at least in order for them to die in every cycle of their lives. so i do that, but, of course, all my neighbors have it, too; so they're all scorching their bedding and shrinking their clothes in the hottest way possible. naturally, the creaky machines in the basement crawling with roaches break in the middle of it all. as i hold back a scream that could echo for a thousand years, there's a blackout. not that it matters as much, i suppose, since my electricity was set to be shut off anyway.

yeah, yeah, i'm wrapping it up. all to say that i can't afford to go to laundry heaven at $3.75 a load. i'm crying my eyes out as i speak. do you know if Laundry Land does low-interest loans?

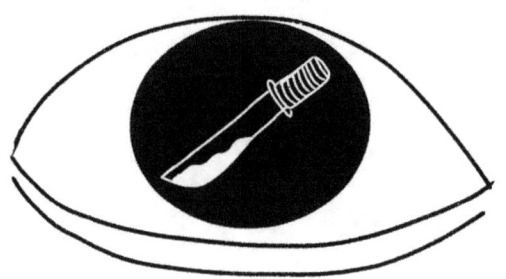

You Know,

I once met a guy like the one on the news—the one that got stabbed to death? Yeah, isn't that wild? I swear he had an odd smile and would go around picking up women left and right, too, just like that guy on the news did. No, he wasn't interested in me or anything, but I think he bought me a drink, and, well—no! Of course, I didn't drink it. But, I guess that pissed him off because his eyes honestly went icicle-cold. Yeah, yeah, he was fit and everything. Had good forearms. That's how you know they're fit. The veins on the forearms burst forward from making a grip too hard with the hands, like you're watching the 3D movie premiere of a superhero film. And you're like, damn, I guess he's fit! Anyway, he didn't do anything to me, but I saw him chatting up some other girls, and they were really fine girls. It bothered me, though, when he kept trying to touch them by being real close, you know, almost up against their backs. Yeah, I know he wasn't as bad as the guy on the news. I just thought they even looked a little similar, too, you know? Haha, yeah, but I'm probably being paranoid. Can you imagine though? Stabbing someone twenty times until they're dead? And, you know, he probably screamed, "I'm sorry I touched those girls! I'm sorry! I'm SO SORRY!" But you know how my imagination runs wild. He's probably at the comfort of his home, falling asleep to the sound of TV static, waiting to be woken up by his too-good-for-him wife in the morning.

Watch Watch Watch

You have always wanted a series of events to happen to you, like some character in a multi-season television show. Your mundane life suddenly dragged into an elaborate plan that only has a little to do with you. Your escape from the clutches of perceived evil, your own heroic fall from grace, followed by a dramatic rise from that rock-bottom, and finally, victory over the evil that had nothing and everything to do with you. The lull and release of tension when an arc is over, only hinting at the next potential issue at the end. What you've wanted is a well-paced plot. But what you realize now is that what you watch and what you feel are actually on either side of a one-way view mirror.

There is an odd sense of disconnect between the program you watch and the camera that's switched on inside of your head. It becomes clear to you that your life would be a heavily edited comedy or an indie film really trying to spell "ennui" in big letters. What the critics would call your agency, or lack thereof, takes the form of molasses. There is nothing written in stone except for the very actions being taken at this exact moment. What you plan and what you actually experience differ so jarringly, that it makes you want to cry. And you do. Then the camera rolls in your head again. A shot of you on the bathroom floor. Crying to someone on the phone. It's comical how such gut-wrenching moments turn into framed shots, how your own life becomes immersed in the language of media. You watch yourself fall apart, take yourself apart, turn into nothing but a puddle, like a crumpled pile of clothes. You wonder if it will always be like this, watching yourself in mild pity from the viewpoint of a surveillance camera, watching yourself limply roll into dirt and dust on the floor. You see yourself crawl into the closet after some time, disappearing from view.

Dearly Departed

We say goodnight and farewell to someone we knew lovingly as Straight Girl Jamie. We find ourselves thinking: why her? Why now? Why so soon? She was taken away from us so quickly by the unraveling of her internalized homophobia, which the doctors can only speculate upon. She flat-lined when she realized how she had loved a girl in middle school, heart thudding against her chest when she kissed her cheek. When she remembered how it felt to dance with the loveliest girl in her class. She nearly left us then, too, tragically hospitalized. She never knew what was coming for her.

And by the time another friend of hers asked years later, "So is Straight Girl Jamie really straight?" she had already been halfway to the other side. I remember her clinging onto a boy, begging to be saved, resuscitated. And I remember when she left him, she had died then, too.

I've seen her shadow like a ghost, lurking in the mirrors when I'm looking down.

I can sometimes feel her, trying to put on my skin when I question myself in the comfort of privacy. I can hear her soft hollow voice whispering to me, "You had a choice, and you chose to kill me."

Let us rejoice that she never left a body.

But I still put on her skin when I see my mother. When I speak to my uncle. When I interact with older family members. She protects me now. I know she is a shield, and I know she is a lie. It's difficult, always putting on a dead person's skin suit in front of those I should fondly call family. But you know how it is; not all truths are meant to be told. At least she hangs beautifully in my closet after a gentle hand washing with mild soap.

Though we bury her today, and we put her to rest as a moment of closure for us all, we will never forget her—or rather, we will never be allowed to forget her. This is not the last time we shall gather. Not the last time I speak of her shifting figure, morphing and distorting through the lens we call memories. She looms with us forever, a haunting that can never quite be cleansed away, never quite shaken off. We put her to rest today, on this sunny afternoon, but she still lives with us—with me— and, I, I feel as though she still sometimes inhabits my body. And I wonder if I am still her after all, even now as we say our tearful goodbyes.

But, worry not dear loved ones. May your souls find gentle peace knowing that I tell her, whenever love threatens to feel uncertain, or a desire is filled with doubt:

"You were never truly alive."

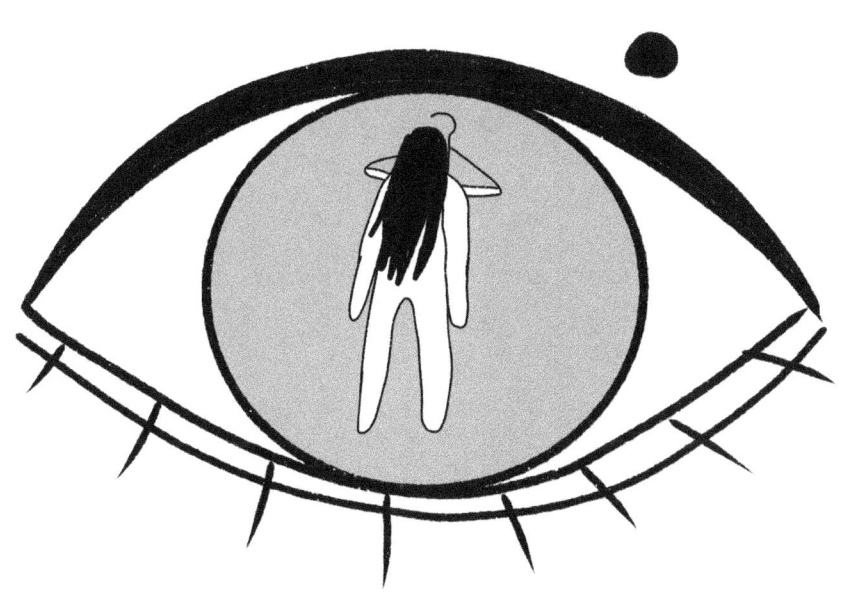

Futuristic

I've heard on the news that it's burning out there. That the particulate matter floating about will hurt your lungs, and I believe it. I've been coughing more than usual, and I've been sneezing several times a row. Which I never do. But some people don't seem all that bothered by it. It doesn't bother me so much either, until I think about it. It's a bit warm for November even for the place where I live. It's warm here all the time, pretty much. But I suppose, even then, it's hard to explain the burning away. But they say, once upon a time, it didn't always burn. They say it happened seasonally, and not even on a yearly basis. But it has always burned for me. It's been burning since I was born, and tourists take pictures of it as they fly on their $200 helicopter tours.

I've been told:

> It must be nice to live somewhere so warm. Look at that view of the California fires. You wouldn't last a day here, south of the equator. Everything is frozen over, so much so that outdoor ice skating rinks are opening up left and right.

So I've said:

> My throat burns. Everything burns. Come feel how real the fires are. How the ash almost glints like glitter as it falls like snow, gently dusting over us like confectioners' sugar, a shaken snow globe with intricate moving parts. And how I don't know a day without burning my retinas when I look out into the distance. The sun has set there and made a home.

How To Fall Apart

```
<!DOCTYPE html>

<html>

<head>

<title>Welcome to Falling Apart!</title>

</head>

<body>

<h2>                        </h2>

    <p>This is how you fall apart. You've heard
    all about meat that falls off the bones. And
    they're not wrong. Not entirely.</p>
    <p>The following represents some of the key
    methods of Falling Apart:</p>

<ul>

    •    <li>Dreams, but no sleep</li>

    •    <li>Love without the beauty</li>

    •    <li>A place that is just out of reach
    (and feeling like you will never ever
    reach it)</li>

</ul>

    <p>The following steps will show you how to
```

do this if you haven't Fallen Apart yet:

<ol>

1.	<li>Already prepared are burdens from your past. Memories that sting to touch, that have been seared so deeply in your mind that it is swollen.</li>

2.	<li>Bottle them all up until they rot. Refuse rescue.</li>

3.	<li>Eventually you will explode. This is simply inevitable, but you will do so under circumstances that will certainly make you look "insane." And maybe you are.</li>

4.	<li>Fall apart when you cannot explain logically how you arrived at this moment. You will hit rock bottom as meat and bones come apart. Then you are ready.</li>

</ol>

Below is a picture of you before this journey:

<a href="https://imgur.com/a/6v7Qs3u" target="_blank"><img src="https://imgur.com/RNjTd0L" alt="Two pieces of delicious BBQ ribs"/></a>

</body>

</html>

Techmate

hello there.

my name is M. M as in, Merry Christmas, Marital, Mobius, etc.

you can ask me anything. just say, "hey M," and i'll be right there.

but first, what's your name?

X

i see! hello, X. that's a lovely name.

why don't you try saying, "hey M, what is the weather forecast for today?"

hey M whats the weather like today

cloudy! with a chance of *murder*

haha, just kidding! it's going to rain starting at 4:03 PM.

remember—if you ever need me, just say, "hey M," and i'll be happy to help!

—

hey M

hi, X! what can i do for you today? you can try saying "tell me the weather" or "call m—

where is the nearest hardware store

here are the nearest hardware stores in your area!

it looks like there's one less than a mile away.

Orchard's Supply Hardware Store
(0.4 mi)
201 Swing Ave
Hours: Open Now

Home Depot
(2 mi)
1158 S Kingsley St
Hours: Open Now

Hard Work Pays Off
(0.0 mi)
8986 Morality St
Hours: OPEN NOW

the last one is a little mood booster!*

*questions about this? feel free to ask them by saying "feedback for M!"

—

hey, X! just reminding you about that meeting you're having in 15 min! if you're running late or if the meeting got pushed back, just slide down the alarm, and set another time!

—

hey M, change my name to xylophone

…are you SURE you want to proceed?

haha, just kidding! just changed your name to xylophone.

[laughing face]*

*questions about this? feel free to ask them by
saying "feedback for M!"

feedback for M. stop making jokes about my name

thank you for giving feedback, xylophone!

we will take this into consideration for our future answers. thanks!

—

hey, xylophone! i see that you have made an *alarming* amount
of purchases for the following items:

- Bleach (knock-off version tho)

- Waterproof tarps

- Shovels (like two of them, but still)

according to the user agreement you signed with us, any
suspicious activities may be shared with our trusty third-party
partners. just letting you know! [heart]

—

hey, xylophone! you are going in the opposite direction of your
morning commute.

would you like to reroute?

—

hey, xylophone! i noticed that you recently deleted our conversation history. (awww...) did you mean to do that?

—

[Phone has been powered off.]

Down the Street, a Little Girl

There is a child in your neighborhood. A perfectly normal looking child who seems to have many normal seeming friends and normal appearing parents. Normal.

A memory loops in your mind. The one time you remember encountering this child, a brief moment you can't quite shake. You walked by her once, at a grocery store seemingly by chance. She was looking at a row of cleaning supplies when someone called her from the next aisle over and she walked past you.

You can't remember her name.

And you caught a whiff of a scent that made you recoil, nearly forcing you to drop the keyring in your right hand. Something fruity with a hint of something rotting underneath. The little girl bounded away, out of sight, presumably reunited with her guardian already. You looked around, wondering if there was a spill nearby or a misplaced package of meat on the shelf. You couldn't spot anything of the sort, and the gut-churning stench was gone as quickly as it had overwhelmed you.

You kept taking deep breaths, sniffing the air to see if you could smell it again, but it was to no avail. So you moved on with your day, looking for the dry foods aisle, for a specific brand of oatmeal.

For some reason, you think of that child now, wondering absentmindedly if she is all right.

—

She wakes up to the same ceiling everyday. Small star stickers all over the wall, faded but it's always there. When she looks around there's a pile of unwashed laundry next to a pile of papers. Her schoolwork.

And next to her is the bed she barely remembers using, currently occupied by a disorderly mountain of miscellaneous items—some in cardboard boxes and others simply piled on top of each other. Figurines, ribbons, clothes, pencil and pen—and more clothes. There was a time when she remembers being able to squeeze into the corner of the bed next to all of the things.

These days she sleeps on the floor. But even that space is growing smaller, too.

The only thing that really bothers her is the fact that she can see straight through the underside of the bed frame. And every time she looks, she can see that one life-size doll that mom brought home one day. She remembers her mom saying, "Look at this lovely doll I got from a yard sale, isn't it just lovely?"

Before she could respond, mom had walked away, wading and squeezing past canyons of boxes full of wares, parts, and clothes, to the small path that leads to her spot by the computer, where she would spend the majority of her time.

But she didn't think the doll was lovely. Its eyes were wide and empty.

After a few months, the doll was placed on the bed. Then, as more stuff piled up, the doll was pushed over to make room, sliding and sliding, until it fell with the loudest thump to the floor she had heard in her life. Ever since then, the doll simply lies still on the floor, under the bed where she can see it nightly, lying there on top of something red. Some nights, she locks eyes with that thing, and sleep doesn't come.

—

In the upcoming days, as if summoned by your memories, the little girl can be seen again outside.

You always wondered if she only plays with those kids in the neatly kept front yard. She has a knack for seeming to blend in, but somehow sticking out at the same time. The other children laugh and play with each other, and she tries, too, but it's hard to say that they actively include her. Rather, she is just there, in attendance, rather than fully participating.

One of the children approaches her and tells her something, fiddling with a small ball between their hands while doing so. You can't hear what they said at all—I mean, how could you, being so far away?

But you can almost see something fall into her, a weight that gives her a blank pause as the other child walks away, carefree in all of their sparkling, wholesome childhood. And she steps slowly away, a hesitant, lost backwards step as she separates herself from the group. A few feet of distance never looked so lonesome as she sits on the ground seemingly alone, playing with the grass.

—

Don't be afraid. Don't be afraid. Don't be afraid.

She knows it's a mantra that never works. She knows that it's supposed to be just a doll, but it's always the what-ifs that suddenly turn her into a statue, like the ones she's seen at the museum a month ago. She thought: *But if I can be still and suddenly move, what if the doll can, too?*

She tears her gaze away from the doll, looking back down at her page of math homework. She is on the floor, belly down, using a hardcover book as a flat surface for her math packet. All desks had already been overtaken by miscellaneous boxes filled with unopened letters and coupons for "clipping later," as mom put it.

What time will it be in 15 minutes?

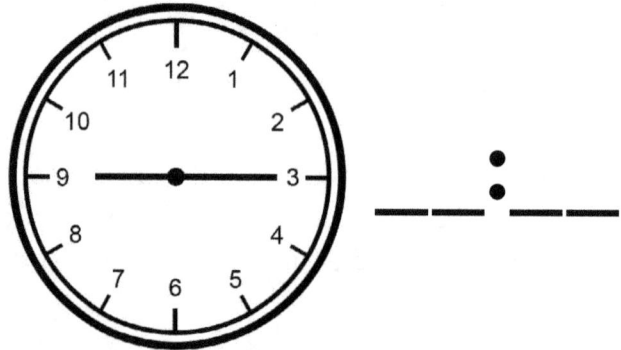

Focusing on the page, she tries to remember the way Ms. Haze explained it. 15 minutes is five, ten, fifteen… It should be 9:30. She writes 9:30 in the blank spaces.

She feels a bit calmer. The house is dead silent aside from distant sounds from the street, someone calling to someone else and they respond. Call and response. She does that at school, too. Ms. Haze says,

If you can hear the sound of my voice, clap once.

If you can hear the sound of my voice, clap twice.

Before she knows it, she is smiling to herself, feeling like she's back in the classroom, sitting at her seat, clapping her hands.

She moves onto the next question and the next and the next until the clocks and numbers blur, multiply, and triple before her eyes. She nods off slowly, although trying to refocus on the page.

Her head feels so heavy, like the heaviest thing in the world, and trying to keep it upright feels unnaturally difficult. She then hears something fall inside the room.

The sound makes her blink slowly. It must have been something from the desk or the many box towers in the room. After some moments of silence, she reassures herself and draws her attention back to the page. Almost on instinct, she looks under the bed again.

She blinks. Her throat runs dry and the feeling of something sinking into her chest, into her stomach follows.

The doll is gone.

Her breathing quickens into a panic, mouth gulping for air as tears begin welling in her eyes. Frantically, she looks around, not wanting to see the doll but at the same time, trying to find it.

She gets up and tries to run out of the bedroom, into the living room, but she trips over a spilled pile of clothes hangers still in their packaging that no one bothered to pick up or use. Her harsh breathing breaks into sobs, fear and anger both leaking out of her eyes as she tries to get up.

Why. Why. Why.

As she weeps, a voice behind her says, "Hey, are you okay?"

She turns her head to look.

—

It's been a nice few days of clear skies with little to no clouds.

The day is pristine, almost too clean, where not a single cloud in the sky obscures the vast blue above. Normally, you don't have much of a thought about a day like this—it's just a nice day.

But, uneasiness bubbles internally, as though you are sitting in the calm before something terrible happens.

As usual, you are looking outside at the bright green lawns. The neighborhood is relatively quiet, aside from the occasional people out walking their dogs, chatting on the phone, or otherwise walking by. You raise your hand at a few of the people you recognize.

Maybe it's the coffee you had earlier causing the jitters that haven't worked their way out of your system yet.

But, in all honesty, you already know what's bothering you. It's been a few days, almost a week now, since you've seen that little girl.

And you used to see her all the time outside, trying so hard to play with the others. And you used to see her, here and there, wandering around.

It's probably nothing. Presumably, and logically, she is simply finding other children to play with. And who knows, maybe she even moved away as the school semester came to a close.

You shift in your seat. Taking a long look at the place where the little girl used to be, you keep glancing around as though expecting her to step back into frame, alive and well, hoping her arrival will quell that hammering fear in your chest.

—

The little girl looks back at the voice behind her. She sees a small girl, just about her age and height standing and staring back at her with wide eyes.

"Did I scare you?"

The little girl, who was still on the ground, having fallen down in an attempt to run, suddenly pauses. Panic slowly subsides, and confusion takes its place. *Where did she come from?*

Before she can say anything at all, the unfamiliar girl continues, "What's your name?" The unfamiliar girl stoops down next to where the little girl had fallen, the unfamiliar girl crossing her arms over her knees.

"My name is…" the little girl replies, blinking, almost like she forgot for a second. "Marla."

"Hi, Marla." The unfamiliar girl looks to be around her age and is wearing a plain, suspender dress with pleats layered over a short-sleeve, Peter Pan-collar blouse. Her shoes are shiny, like one of those dress-up Mary Jane shoes for dolls. The lace and bow around her ruffle socks are delicate and clean. "My name is Cally. It's so nice to meet you!"

Cally doesn't look like she belongs in this house. She appears to be the sole existence in color, the only one that is alive with her well-pressed skirt pleats and starched white shirt. Marla looks down at her own clothes and sees a stain that she didn't realize was there before. Looks almost big, and red.

After a long moment, Marla says, in a small voice, "Hi, Cally."

—

"Do you like to climb mountains, Cally?"

"Um… I've tried before, but it didn't go so well."

"Oh, that's okay! Here, I'll show you how I do it."

The little girls pack what little they have to begin their ascent to the mountain called Stone Red. Under their feet are boxes, dolls, candles, laundry, books, and letters—so many letters. The road ahead is harsh and dangerous, but they are determined. Cally follows in Marla's steps, stepping carefully up the plastic bags puffy and bloated with clothes. There's also an industrial-sized laundry basket underneath the mountain, propping it up.

"I love climbing up here, to the top of Mt. Stone Red, and see everything become small below."

Cally is a bit quiet all of a sudden, her vibrancy dulling with every step up Mt. Stone Red. Grabbing a loose graphic tee sticking out from a box, they suddenly feel the mountain shaking. They feel the mountain keeling, about to fall towards them before Marla leans forward, stabilizing the movement. Cally screams, almost bursting into tears. "No! No!" *She is grabbing onto the mountain, for dear life.* "I don't want to go anymore. I don't want to go to the top. I'm heading back down."

"What?" *Marla looks back down at her.* "Why not? We're almost there."

"I don't feel good," *Cally says suddenly, looking down. She looks so, so pale.* "I don't want to go up."

"Maybe you're scared of heights, Cally." *Marla tries to flash Cally a smile, but she isn't looking up.* "Once you're up there, it's gonna be awesome. Everything looks far away and small. And from there, if you just look to the right–"

"No, I don't want to see that." Cally goes still, very still, as though deciding if she should run to the bathroom to throw up or not. "No, no, no, no, no. I have to lie down. I'm going back down."

"Uh, okay." Marla says, worried. "I'll be back down really quick."

Cally climbs back down, slowly, and she slumps away, lying down, clutching her middle. She crawls over, looking like she wants to get on the bed. But there's no room to lie down on the mattress.

She crawls under the bed, groaning in pain. Cally screams as she spies a cockroach crawling at full speed towards her, and she bangs her head hard against the bed frame above her. Cally starts crying, sobs rattling through her small body, as though only now realizing her misfortune.

Marla is still climbing, perhaps not having heard Cally at all. She climbs up another box full of dirtied toys and creased playing cards. Eventually, Marla reaches the top, having climbed all the way up. "Look, Cally! It wasn't so bad after all."

Marla searches for Cally, having a full view of the land below, at the very top of Mt. Stone Red. "Cally?" Marla calls out. But she is only met with silence.

[LOOK AROUND MARLA

LOOK AROUND YOU

I AM RIGHT HERE DON'T YOU RECOGNIZE

ME

DON'T YOU RECOGNIZE

YOUR OWN

MOTHER]

Marla suddenly hears Cally crying from somewhere near the bed, maybe under it. "Cally? Cally, I'm sorry. I forgot you're feeling sick. I'm gonna go get my mom."

Cally continues to cry, sobbing and sniffling like she's full of snot and tears all over. Marla can think of all the words that mean "to cry," and she can hear that Cally is doing all of them. Only her sobs fill the dreadful silence, and Marla can feel the sadness fill her own heart. "Please don't cry, Cally." Her voice breaks a bit, helplessness falling into her limbs and feet, just like the time she fell over while running from this very room.

It feels like it's been ages ago since that happened.

"Where is your mom, Marla?!" Cally screams out.

"She's…" Marla glances over at the corner of the room.

Where the doll used to be.

It's the place where she last saw mom, looking like a stone and red. She's a black swirl now, filled with buzzing.

—

It is a lovely blue day, until you hear the sirens rushing through the neighborhood.

At first, it doesn't seem like that big of a deal. Until a bit later, when the police cars also head in the same direction. You step out onto your porch, looking toward the direction of the speeding vehicles. A few neighbors have also come out to take a look. Dread pools into your stomach.

You try to see where the cars are going, and they turn the corner. You feel yourself rushing out of the house, feet hitting the pavement, in a hurry; worried, unsettled.

The little girl down the street isn't too far. When you jog along this street, you know where she lives. You run over, like you did something wrong. You know you didn't. But maybe you did.

You get to the place, and the entire block of homes seem to be abuzz, watching from their homes. The caution tape and men in uniforms stop you in your tracks. You can't go any closer, but there is someone on a stretcher being taken away. From your limited vantage point, the figure seems to be an adult.

After some time, all the neighborhood's eyes go toward the house's door—a child coming out on a stretcher. For the briefest moment, you can see her looking around before a paramedic approaches her and guides her to the ambulance.

—

You didn't see her again.

But the rumors spread and became the talk of the small community, as though it were simply some gossip from tabloids. Some talk about how they knew that there had to be something wrong, having lived there long enough to know that they rarely had guests over.

Another time, a child had talked a bit about how she had a "smell" to her. All the little snippets in the world—how she had been seen here and there, showing up in strangely stained clothes, or having not seen her mom in a long while.

Pity and gossip, like fog settling in on a cold night, surround this child, whose name you still do not know.

And whatever happened in that house? Well, the local news later reported that a child was found in a hoarder's house, alongside a dead body revealed to be a child who did not belong to the hoarder.

You wonder where she is now, in the comfort of your clean home.

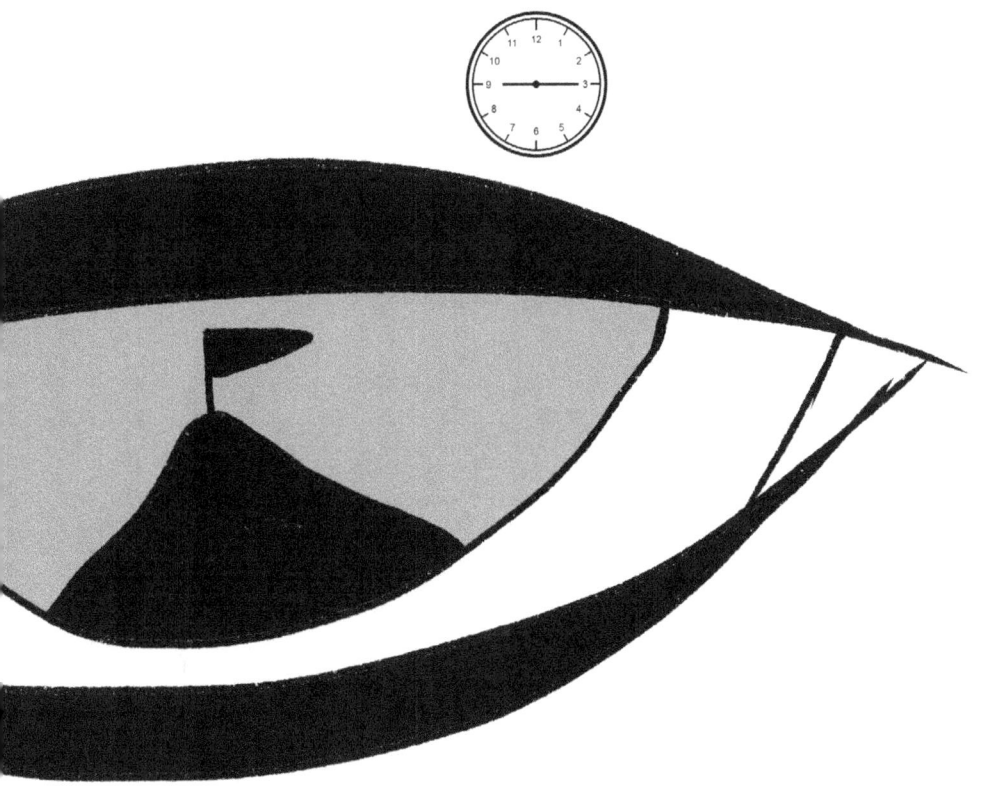

time is felt, not measured

open up a bottle of Garnier Fructis shampoo, and i'm right there in the hallways of my school.

funny how memories like these filter it all for you, capture a long-lost moment that echoes as an ache in your chest. is it longing or is it loss? was it really all that beautiful? going back in the shoes of your younger self, it would not feel the same. even if you could jump back in time as yourself, it is all the more likely that you would prefer smelling that fragrance of a memory secretly in the aisle of a CVS (not recommended).

memories fade into blotted stains in your mind, distilling a feeling of what once was, not as it was. filtered in sepia and blurred for your enjoyment now, for the you who is grown up and so different, yet still exactly the same. a moment that captures the you now and the you then.

it is a blessing to be able to experience that feeling of traveling through time.

oh, how you have survived. you who trudged here to the present, day by day. it is the you in youth that chose to continue. it is the same you that marked the distance between you now and the you then.

maybe even unwillingly.

the waves of nostalgia mark again and again the immeasurable growth between these two selves, in two different times. you would not be here, in the now, to indulge in the past should you not have gone through it.

i inhale that fragrance—soapy-clean, bubbly-synthetic. and my heart aches, not for loss or longing, I realize, but for where i came from and where i am now. i am safe enough to indulge in that mixture of pain and joy safely, in the comfort of the present.

nostalgia is a gift to yourself, a myriad of heartaches and joys, however small, that you can only enjoy because you have lived.

because you are here.

the end?

from the way the light hits your eye, i get the feeling
that it's time for us to go.
and even though i am holding you
and you are holding me
it's fleeting.
really, such a small moment in our lifetimes.

and maybe you won't remember how you met me,
and maybe you will put me back where you found me
and maybe you will go on
on and on
and i'll be but a fractured remnant of a bygone era.

but i don't mind—i don't mind at all.

even as I exist here
longing,
i know you will find what you need
out there.

but it's not like i don't have small amounts of greed in my heart.
i'll secretly hope that (or maybe i'll pretend)
that you have taken a piece of me with you
far, far away through every inevitable scrape and bump of life.

and maybe, just maybe
well, in my wishful mind,
years down the line
you will remember me,
as though recalling a long-lost dream.

perhaps you will remember a feeling,
and if you ever fall for that longing,
that little ache,
you can always reach for me, for my words.
but until that day, i will miss you.

i love you—please don't forget me.

About the Author

Jeongmin "Jamie" Choi is a Korean writer based in Tongva land, also known as Los Angeles, California.

Born in Seoul, South Korea, before moving to her current location in the United States, she began her foray into art at the age of seven via dance. Simultaneously, she also had to learn English quickly in order to communicate with her peers. By middle school, she had begun dabbling in storytelling via short stories and drawings as a hobby.

In high school, her experiences were split into two—that of the high achieving student and that of a burned out student struggling with both depression and anxiety. In such a conflicting state, she opted to continue her education by enrolling at the University of California, Los Angeles with a major in English. Within a much larger school setting, thriving was difficult, and her mental health declined drastically, becoming unable to continue with classes for a time being. Much of her experiences from the mental health struggles from this period of her life inform the tone and aesthetic of her works.

Through much effort, she returned to university and eventually was able to finish her degree, B.A. in English. Many questions arose for her during this time, especially regarding the validity and moral integrity of hierarchical structures, such as racism, sexism, ableism, and much more. Having thought deeply about the nuances of mental health, difficulties of recovery, and the need for survival, her writing style has evolved into one that asks readers to question and re-imagine their belief systems and the material structures of their reality.

She now writes short stories, flash fiction, and poetry that attempt to capture a sense of magic, surreality, and horror to highlight the unseen and unheard, integrating optimism and harsh reality in new, exciting ways.

Her works have been featured in independent press such as *Mixed Mag Co.*, and *Third Iris Zine*. She also researched and presented a creative writing and local history workshop called *The Potential of Transit,* as a part of DSTL Arts' Creative Impact series in February 2024.

You can find her works via the QR code or at *https://linktr.ee/whisperlanding.*

She is also on Instagram as *@whisperlanding.*

Acknowledgments

I would like to thank all of the people who have supported me thus far. First and foremost, I reserve much of my gratitude to DSTL Arts for helping me throughout the process of creating this chapbook every step of the way. Specifically, I thank you Angie, Luis Antonio Pichardo, and Abraham Jaramillo for putting in so much effort into the creation of this chapbook.

Thank you especially to my mom, Jina Han, for the steady, unyielding support she has shown me over so many years. Without her financial and mental support, there is no telling what could have happened to me. I am grateful for her patience and will always admire her willingness to learn in some capacity, regardless of age.

And of course, thank you to all of my loved ones, friends, and chosen family. I cannot emphasize enough how near and dear all of you are to my heart, and that it would not be an exaggeration to say that this body of work is for you all. The countless moments of encouragement, uplifting of my spirits, and pure love that I have been blessed enough to experience in this lifetime is immeasurable. I only hope that I can return the energy in kind.

Thank you to those who have also purchased a copy of the chapbook or obtained it in some other way. Your support means the world to me, and I hope that it has been a meaningful journey for you overall.

Well, until next time.
— Jeongmin "Jamie" Choi

DSTL
arts

This publication was produced by DSTL Arts.

DSTL Arts is a nonprofit arts mentorship organization that inspires, teaches, and hires emerging artists from underserved communities.

To learn more about DSTL Arts, visit online at:

DSTLArts.org
@DSTLArts

www.ingramcontent.com/pod-product-compliance
Lightning Source LLC
Chambersburg PA
CBHW051146020726
47501CB00005B/1705